This book belongs to:

. . . .

. . . .

For Leroy

and his story

Also with love and thanks to my friends –

Tricia, Melanie,

Frank (especially for co-editing late at night in Cork),

Carolyn, Kate, Helen,

Paul and Sybille

and to Mark and Bonzo across the alleyway

Also to Cathryn

*This story is based in and around
Salisbury Road and Beaumont Park,
Plymouth. Ordinary life.
Warmest thanks to Michael Hill
and to Helen Read at Walker Books.*

To find out more about
Simon James and his books visit
www.simonjamesbooks.com

First published 1997 by Walker Books Ltd
87 Vauxhall Walk, London SE11 5HJ

This edition published 2008

10 9 8 7 6 5

© 1997, 2003, 2008 Simon James

The right of Simon James to be identified as author/illustrator
of this work has been asserted by him in accordance with
the Copyright, Designs and Patents Act 1988

This book has been typeset in Goudy

Printed in China

British Library Cataloguing in Publication Data:
a catalogue record for this book is
available from the British Library

ISBN 978-1-4063-0849-5

www.walker.co.uk

SIMON JAMES

Leon and Bob

WALKER BOOKS
AND SUBSIDIARIES
LONDON · BOSTON · SYDNEY · AUCKLAND

Leon had moved into town
with his mum.
His dad was away in the army.
Leon shared his room with
his new friend, Bob.

No one else could see Bob
but Leon knew he was there.
Leon always laid a place
for Bob at the table.
"More milk, Bob?" Leon said.

Sometimes Leon's mum
couldn't take Leon to school,
but Leon didn't mind.
He always walked to school with Bob.
He always had Bob to talk to.

Often, when Leon got home,
there was a letter waiting for him
from his dad.
Bob liked to hear Leon read it
over and over again.

One Saturday, Leon heard
some noises in the street below.
He saw a new family moving in
next door.
A boy looked up at Leon and waved.
Leon waved back.

That night Leon kept thinking
about the boy next door.
He decided to go round there
in the morning.
"But you'll have to come with
me, Bob," he said.

The next day Leon and Bob
ate their breakfast
very quickly.
Then Leon grabbed his ball
and rushed outside.

Leon ran up the steps
of next-door's house.
He was about halfway
when suddenly he realized
Bob wasn't there any more.

Leon sat down.

He was all alone.

He could ring the bell

or he could go home.

Why wasn't Bob there

to help him?

Leon rang the bell
and waited.
The door opened.
"Hello," said the boy.
"H-hello," said Leon.
"Would you like to go to the park?"

"OK," said the boy.

"I'm just going to the park, Mum,"
he called.

Together Leon and the boy walked
down the steps towards the street.

"My name's Leon," said Leon.

"What's yours?"

"Bob," said Bob.

SIMON JAMES

Simon James is an award-winning author and illustrator of books for children – creator of the much-loved character Baby Brains and of touching tales exploring a child's unique relationship with Nature.

ISBN 978–1–4063–4103–4

ISBN 978–1–4063–0845–7

ISBN 978–1–4063–0848–8

ISBN 978–1–4063–0846–4

ISBN 978–1–4063–0849–5

ISBN 978–1–84428–467–2

ISBN 978–1–84428–522–8

ISBN 978–1–4063–0202–8

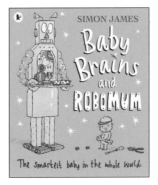

ISBN 978–1–4063–1338–3

"Drawing always opens up a very private and delightful world. It's easy to forget that drawing in itself is a kind of magic. Drawing is good for you!" SIMON JAMES

Available from all good booksellers
www.walker.co.uk